TEENAGE

I AM DOG

Anne Santos

Pen Press

First published in Great Britain by
Pen Press an Imprint of Indepenpress
25 Eastern Place
Brighton
BN2 1GJ

ISBN 978-1-906710-54-5

Printed and bound in the UK

A catalogue record of this book is available from
the British Library

Cover design Jacqueline Abromeit
Illustrations by Patrice Palmer
Thanks to Maria Sanderson for the use of her photography
as models for the illustrations

For the two of them

About the Author

Annette de Burgh Santos was born and educated in Liverpool. After a brief spell in nursing she took a course in Journalism and Commercial Art before moving to Bearsden, Glasgow. Here she became involved in many voluntary organisations including Glasgow Samaritans, The Children's Hearing System (Juvenile Court) and served as a Magistrate for the city of Glasgow.

At a dog centre she found Seth, with whom many invigorating rambles were enjoyed with her family, exploring some spectacular countryside.

Now living in Warwickshire, England. Anne and is currently involved with various local activities. She is published writer of poetry, articles and short stories. "I am Dog" is her first published book.

Contents

Contents

Spring

*"… and the earth was without form and
void … the darkness was upon
the face of the deep."*

D arkness. There is no light, just a cloaking clinging darkness and unknown sounds everywhere! Feeble yelps and cries, the crunch of heavy boots on straw.

Feelings: the rough tongue cleaning my coat; the soft belly giving me warmth; a teat in the mouth giving me food.

Helplessness. I totter unsteadily, wobbling on my short, thin legs and fall on the damp straw.

I push and yell for my share of the milk. I grow. No longer do I need poor old Tess, who has whelped so many over the years. She is tired and worn, aged from suckling pups.

Big Ben, a champion amongst Border Collies, sired me. He is a dog who knows instinctively about sheep and men, who can coax a stupid, stubborn ewe from pen to pen, so noiselessly, so speedily, yet so very gently. Big Ben, who obeys nature, and man's whistle. Such beauty, such perfection, such grace on the hillside; such bounty gained in trophies for men to house.

Now I crawl nearer to Tess. Her coat is matted with dirt. She lies panting and in pain on the putrid straw, unkempt and uncared for.

So, this is my life, for I know of no other.

Knowing only the darkness, I have no fear. I have no worries. I know not envy. I know not jealousy. I know neither love nor hate. I am neither depressed nor dissatisfied. I can anticipate only my next breath.

And always the darkness except, so briefly, so very briefly, the daily shaft that flashes joyously across the shed when the old door creaks open, shattering through the gloom. In that instant, the dirty straw takes on a golden glow, for *tis then fools' gold*.

Dirty mud-caked boots stomp uncaringly, ploughing through the dross, and we scurry in apprehension. A small, chipped enamel bowl is thrown carelessly into a corner offering a brief meal of maize. We push, pant and fight to get a share, grabbing and snarling for the miserable, inadequate food. And yet, I am satisfied. I have nothing with which I can compare this existence called living.

Tess, when she has the energy and inclination, talks

of green fields, and the smell of sheep and lambs, of long hard runs into the waiting hills. She tells us about swishing, welcoming grass, soft gentle rain on the coat, and a day's work well done. We hear about streams and trees, shade and shadows on a summer's day, cool mountain water, falling leaves and frost beneath the paws, and a light, white, bright snow.

But they are only empty words. All I know is the darkness, the smell and the loneliness. This shed is my world.

Tess dies. Suddenly, silently and without complaint, through age, lack of care, too much hard work, and too many pups. There have been cold days when she has shivered for too long, her black coat wet with rain and heavy with clinging mud, the white pride of her bib a dull grey. She dies, as she had learned to live – in a shed.

Poor Tess.

Poor weary Tess. Her days of mist, mountains, showers, shade and sun, gone; her pup-filled hours, past; her memories of sheep-white hills, and youthful runs, far away; her sorrow and her sadness – no more. All just a thought – a memory.

"What will happen to us?" It is all we can wail through the long, lonely night in the dark shed.

Squabbles are forgotten. Needful, we huddle together in

a common cause for warmth. Companionship comes from necessity, protection from need. Unity is now our strength. Oneness is a strange feeling, and fear is with us.

We push into the cold, stiff body of Tess. But she gives us no comfort. We nuzzle her, crying together for an answer.

Fear comes stealthily into the shed. There is darkness, and the shed is all night. Hunger grips our small bellies. We forage in the straw, trying to eat the thin stalks. We scrape at the enamel bowl, but no small morsel clings to its rim.

A loud banging comes from outside. An angry voice yells harshly, "Shut up!"

Frightened we stop crying. There is an eerie quietness. We moan gently together; it is the lullaby of our fatigue and fear. Then, exhausted, we sleep.

A creaking awakens us and we yelp in surprise. Boots push us aside, without thought or care.

"The bitch is dead," a voice announces, without feeling. They stand by the still, stiff form that once was Tess.

"Well, she did her job to the last. She produced a fair litter. Mind you, that one's not up to much." The boot digs into my belly.

They drag Tess out. She has served man and they have no use for her now. Her weight parts the damp straw; the stench rises.

"Phew!" they say as she is thrown uncaringly outside the shed.

The shaft of brightness widens and I see light. It dazzles me with its brilliance. I smell a sweet smell and it overpowers me with its fragrance. I hear a bird singing and it uplifts me with its song.

"Shut the door, we don't want the buggers out."

The door bangs. Again the darkness returns.

But now I have seen light. I have smelled fresh air. I have heard a joyous song. My world has changed.

"What is outside?" the rest ask me.

"Light," I reply, "and life."

"We know nothing," they whisper. "What are these things of which you talk?"

"Light comes from somewhere above, it is beyond description. The sweet smell is a memory of what Tess talked about, and the noise of a bird is the sound of freedom. We should seek the light, the air and the music."

"We know only this shed." They move away. "We cannot face outside. We would surely perish."

"No, we would live," I argue.

Now I know a feeling that invades my contentment. Once I lived in ignorance, but now I have seen, I have smelled and I have heard. There is light, air and sound.

"Oh, what will become of us?" we all wail far into the night.

Without Tess we are rudderless. We fight, we yelp long and loud. No one bothers. We receive our maize and water. There is no change in our miserable lives.

The door creaks open. We cringe. The light comes in.

A heavy boot at my rump. A coarse hand picks me up by the scruff. I growl as best I can, but it is pathetically lost as I am swung high into space. My belly is squeezed. My ears poked. My eyes examined. My mouth prodded with a dirty finger. I close my jaws.

"Ouch!" a voice snarls.

I am dropped violently onto the straw. I give a whimper of pain and bare my teeth in mock self-defence.

"He's a bad-tempered son of a bitch."

I lie down, watching the others sidle round the boots.

I give a faint growl for attention.

"Shut up."

"I'll take these two." A hand points to the two who huddle at the boots.

I see them go out to the light, the air, and the sound. I cry in the darkness, and know both envy and jealousy.

That night there are loud, scaring noises of unknown violence outside. We crouch and huddle nearer for comfort, for we are fewer in number now.

"Get in there!" The door bursts open, but there is no shaft of gentle light, just noise, darkness and the rushing of an angry wind, complaining and blowing the straw into a strange dance round the shed.

"Go on, get in." The voice is gruff.

Something is shoved into the shed. We smell him before we see him. It is Big Ben. Wearily he moves through the straw. We nuzzle into his coat. He is cold, wet and muddy. He rises to shake droplets from his coat. His tail is ragged with mud, and he attempts to part it by licking at the matted hairs.

"What is that noise?" we ask.

"The wind and the rain," he growls.

"Why are you so wet?"

"I was on the hills finding the lost lambs for the shepherd."

"Were you not frightened?"

"No." His voice has grown kindlier. "There is nothing to fear in the wind and the rain. Man is all you have to fear."

"Man?" we ask.

"Yes, man. The wind and rain are fierce but fair. The snow is cold, but soft and gentle. Man is cold and hard, unjust and cruel. Man is unknown even unto himself. There is nothing to compare with his wrath. There is little he will not destroy; there is little he loves."

"Does he beat you?"

"No, man cannot afford to beat me," Big Ben replies. "If I am ill, who will tend to his sheep?"

He staggers up and moves round and round in a circle, making the straw turn with him. He settles down in the midst of it, like a ring with nose buried in tail.

Now he sighs, exhausted. "This straw is damp." It is a statement not a complaint. "Is it ever changed?"

"No, it is always like this," we answer.

"Well, you will be away soon." His voice is tired. "The time has come to sell you."

"Where will we go?"

"Some to farmers, some to shepherds, some, well …" he pauses. "You will have to learn to work, obey and serve. Your life will be as you make it. You may look up to the hills with pride, or down at the mud with discontent."

"Will they sell you, Big Ben?" I ask.

He shakes his head and I see his intelligent eyes stare into mine.

"They will not sell me. You do not sell your breakfast to pay for your dinner."

I do not understand – not yet.

*

The Awakening

*"Let there be light
... and there was light."*

The shed door swings open.

There are voices and boots. I growl, but I am not heeded. The others are taken out, quickly. I have no time to wonder. Hands grab me. The voices are loud. Then suddenly there is quietness; the yelps and whines have ceased.

I am pushed roughly under an arm. Then there is light, sight, and joy! Above is this brilliance and a breeze blows kindly through my fur. I sniff. I smell the sweetness of life. I see. I breathe the air.

There is a flapping and a shrill cry. My ears shoot up. My eyes see, and my nose twitches. I yelp in surprise and gladness. A hand cuffs me.

There is space and no darkness. I am apprehensive, but not afraid. I have knowledge of the light because I have known the darkness. I see moving trees clapping hands to the sky. I see hills kissing the clouds. I smell the glory of the earth. It is beautiful. I smell the green of it; I see the blue of it; I hear the joy of it. Is this freedom?

Another shed. I cry in anguish. Dim, not the darkness, but not the light. I am thrown onto the straw. I wriggle. It is soft and dry. It does not have the acrid smell, but the smell of an unknown. I am alone.

I crouch and wait before crawling tentatively on my belly. The straw tickles. I jump. I scratch at the wooden walls and see my claw marks faintly.

I hear a chomp, chomp and I smell the smell of animals. I give a faint pitiful bark. Chomp, chomp. It is a muffled, unknown sound. I sniff, and smell wood, straw and sweat.

"Little dog, be quiet," a booming voice neighs.

I lie, cowed. "Are you a dog?" I ask timidly.

"I am a horse. I am strong. I serve man."

The chomping continues. I am lonely. I miss the darkness, for it was my friend then. The light is an enemy, it disturbs. I was in ignorance, but now I have the beginnings of knowledge.

My time in the stall does not last. I am dragged out into the light and see the beauty of the dawn of a day.

"Sit down, you stupid mutt," a voice says. A hand brutally knocks me to the ground.

I lie. My eyes are fixed unblinkingly on the boots, and I smell the odour of man. The boots move and slowly I slink in their wake.

I want to run, run into the lush green hills, feel the carpet cool beneath my paws. I want to smell the fresh clean air and the scent of the wildlife. I want to see the light. I want to hear the noise of nature. But I am picked up and thrown into a dirty, smelly cubicle. The door shuts snappily. We move.

The journey ends in another shed; the darkness has returned. As I crawl into the unwelcoming blackness, I sense the other dogs. I smell their uncertainty, their aggression, their anger. They lie silent, still and watchful. My eyes see silhouetted shapes.

"Where am I?" I ask.

"You are with the shepherd."

I see a large old Collie, his coat dark as the gloom. There are other dogs, four in all. They snarl. Tempers are fraught.

"Why am I here?"

"Rejects!" the old dog replies. "Bought by the shepherd who will sell you for what he can get."

"When will that be?"

"When you have learned," the old dog answers.

"And what must I learn?"

"To become biddable," is his reply.

"But what does it mean?"

He sighs.

"Is it important?"

"Learning to survive in man's world is the most important lesson you will ever learn." The answer is grave.

I take little notice as I nose round. My nose twitches at the mixture of new smells. There is musk and earth and dankness, and the pungent aroma of urine. There is no straw now beneath my paw only the hard earth. I try and scratch at the unfamiliar earth, but it yields not to my touch.

"What is your name?" I ask the old dog.

"I am called Clyde," he replies. "What do they call you?"

"I have no name."

"Who sired you?"

"I was sired by Big Ben," I answer proudly.

"Then we will call you Baby Ben," he states, losing interest, and I see him wander off and lie down.

I crouch, feeling the growing antagonism in the other dogs. My hair rises and I feel aggression. I smell trouble. I give a growl.

There in the filmy gloom we all exist. It is not living – I know that now, for I have learned there is light. I am no longer contented.

And so, daily I grow. New teeth come painfully on gnawed stones, my fang teeth. I should look fierce.

Our day is broken by the shepherd's visits. He is a poor man who talks to himself.

The other dogs and I run round the shed chasing each other, bored and barking.

"Do not bark," Clyde tells us. "Collies do not scare sheep, they are swift and sure. Barking is for fool dogs. Yapping is for stupid dogs. Silence is for intelligent dogs. We know how to bark, yet know when to bark."

We learn, trying to remember. Shep is boisterous and forgets. Blackie is timid and yaps. Beth is gentle and too trusting. Jake is sleek, sure and confident. I am ambitious.

"You are not watchdogs; you are born for sheep. Remember," Clyde lectures.

I do not seek fights. I watch and I learn.

"Now," Clyde instructs us as we lie at his paws, "the time is coming for you to leave. Your future will depend on what you have learned here in the darkness. A Collie is biddable. Blackie," Clyde says, "you must not be timid or man will oppress you. Shep, do not bark constantly. If man wishes a guard dog, he will buy a German sheepdog. And if he wishes a docile dog, Beth, then he will buy a toy dog. Oh, and Jake, if man wishes an arrogant dog, he will buy a Chow. But if man wishes a companion who is both intelligent and obedient, then he will buy you, or you, or you."

We sit at his paws and gaze into his liquid brown eyes that have seen so much of man's world.

"Remember this lesson," he continues. "Bend with the wind."

"But what does that mean?" we ask, puzzled.

"You growl," Clyde explains patiently to us, "because you feel that is what a dog does. It is not necessary; you do not need to appear brave. Be pleasing, learn to obey through instinct. Do not seek trouble. There is no disgrace in walking away from a fight. Be biddable. Please man.

"Be aggressive and you will receive a beating. Be biddable and you will receive praise. Bend with the wind and you will not break. The oak tree stands tall, straight and proud. But when the wind and the rain come, beating down fiercely, the oak is without strength. It cannot yield, and so it is broken.

"A sapling young and wiser by far, bends and sways and dances and laughs with the wind. It will not break. That is being biddable."

So Clyde talks to us each day, and I now understand.

The shepherd comes, and I run and lick his hand. Shep barks, Jake is arrogant, Beth afraid. They are ignored or cuffed. I am patted. How long, I wonder, will we all remain here in the darkness? Days and nights are but one.

... and hope.

Then the door of the shed swings open, so slowly, and we smell the shepherd, and strangeness.

They come into the shed cautiously. They wear no boots. They step carefully over the ground. I sense their uncertainty. I smell their diffidence. They are different.

"Are these all you have?" a voice asks without interest.

"They are all good dogs, sir." The shepherd is anxious to please.

They hesitate.

"And this one?" A finger points to Clyde.

"He is old, sir," the shepherd replies.

We feel the tension. We smell the nervous apprehension. We start to run round the shed. Shep barks loudly for attention.

"He'd make a good watch-dog, sir." The shepherd points to Shep.

"I don't want a watch-dog," is the reply.

"Well, Beth, she is quiet," the shepherd says. But Beth is too timid and will not come from the corner. They are not interested in Beth. Jake swaggers, confidently across, so sure and so arrogant.

As I remember the light and the sweet smell and sounds, I make my way cautiously to the front of a shoe and stop.

"Oh look, what is this one like?" I hear a boy's young, eager voice.

"That is Baby Ben, he is a good dog." The shepherd pats my head and flattens down my ears. "He is known as a bluey." The stroking continues.

"I don't think there is much here," the deep voice says, and shoes shuffle towards the door.

I lie quietly waiting.

"Ben is a biddable dog, sir." The shepherd hauls me up and I lick his hand.

"Biddable! That's a nice word," the young voice says.

I turn my brown eyes towards him. I smell the friendliness.

"Well, put him down and let's see," the man says.

I am placed outside in the yard and I hear Clyde's voice, "Bend with the wind." I smell the air, I see the trees and the birds sing to me.

I crouch. They inspect my belly, teeth and eyes. I do not make a sound. But now I turn and lie on my back, for it is the position of vulnerability.

I am placed outside in the yard and I hear Clyde's voice, "Bend with the wind." I smell the air, I see the trees and the birds sing to me.

"Oh, I like him, I like him," the young voice cries. "He is gentle and nice."

"Biddable," the shepherd repeats.

"Let's have him, please Dad!"

I have been bought! I am away from the darkness.

"We are not farmers," the man says, "but he will be well cared for."

Young hands pick me up. Gently. I shiver. A hand lightly rubs my ears. There is no time to say goodbye to Clyde who taught me how to be biddable.

*

The Enlightenment

"And God called the light 'day'
and the darkness he called 'night'.
And Adam named his son 'Seth'."

O ut of the darkness.

I come to learn the ways of humans. There is sight, sound and smell, and my horizon stretches daily. But with enlightenment comes the seeds of knowledge, and knowledge brings forth terror.

Darkness then was my friend; her cloak encased me. Light awakens me to thought, there are no folds to protect me.

My shed – gone. Familiar smells – gone. No darkness. I am shown light.

My home is called kennel. It is large but lonely and my world is now surrounded by wire. I learn that light is not freedom. I am still not free.

Now is my time for learning. In the darkness I was ignorant, but I can no longer return. Like the blind beggar that I was – the clay has been pressed on my sightless eyes – now I see.

With my animal intuition, I learn to distinguish by smell the friend from the foe. I learn about man from man.

"You are to be called Seth," the young voice says. "You are son of Adam. Adam was of the earth."

I listen to the sounds. Seth. Seth. It is a good name. Baby Ben was of the shed. Seth is of the light. Yes, I am well pleased.

I am washed in warm, soothing water that runs through my fur and over my eyes, but the hands are tender. I feel the dust of the shed being removed from my coat, and with the familiar smell goes the last thoughts of darkness and my ignorance.

The land that is now mine is named garden. Here, daily, I learn. Not from he who has the young voice, but he who is older and wise, stern but just, and used to obedience. There is a pattern to my days, divided between work and play, and I learn.

"Come! Come!" The choke chain pulls at my neck when I disobey.

"Sit! Sit!"

"Lie! Lie!"

"Stay! Stay!"

"Run! Run!"

"Good Seth. Well done. You are quick to learn."

But I also learn pain inflicted by man, for my good. On a table, experienced hands examine me. A needle: long, sharp, hurtful. I do not cry. This man they call my master, this man who gently rubs my ears, tickles my belly, teaches me, this man I trust. He will not harm me.

My world grows through sight and sound and smell. I learn more of human ways. They are strange ways: sometimes unjust, sometimes cruel, often incomprehensible.

My master, who is strong and good and fair and kind, teaches me through sound to become obedient. He teaches me through hurt if I do not obey. He teaches me through love if I do obey. My master is obedience.

Smell gives me knowledge of the earth, of what is beneath my paws. Smell is my wisdom, it cannot be taught by man.

Smell and sound are my gifts.

The kennel has sweet smelling straw. My belly is filled with good food, my coat is brushed daily and so it shines darkly and gives me pride. I have a collar, and a name tag that says *Seth*.

But I resent the enclosing wire surrounding my kennel. It offends me that they need to make me a prisoner. I play at escaping. It is not difficult, for I am intelligent, and I can climb and gnaw.

"Seth, you are worse than Houdini," the master says crossly.

But I do not run away, I lie outside my prison. So they tear it down, the wire, the poles. Have they also learned the uselessness of a prison?

Now I have a chain, but it allows me freedom, and often they forget to chain me up. I will not wander. There is nowhere for me to go.

Slowly I enter the heart of man. My days are no longer all training, kennel and walks. I have moved quietly into their house. I lie on soft carpets at the feet of my master.

"He is a fine dog," they say of me.

I am clean. I am careful. The house is my master's kennel. I seek corners. I am biddable.

We walk together, the master and I. Now the choke collar is removed from my neck – obedience through pain.

I see the hills in the distance, the space, the limits of my freedom. I drink from cool pools of water in the fork of tree roots. Squirrels mock and tease me from branches above. I do not bark. I am well taught, and not by men.

"He is a fine dog," they say.

My life is good. But sometimes – just sometimes – when I am on a long walk over the hills, I see in the distance a dark, moving speck gathering in the sheep. And sometimes, just sometimes, I just wish …

22

But I have found the light. This, after all, is my life.

I can bend with the wind.

I am biddable.

I am Seth!

*

Summer

*"Verily, verily I say unto you
I am the door of the sheep."*

I know only dogs such as I.

Black dogs with white paws. Border Collies, swift and sure, obedient and loyal, bred for the shepherd, to become minders of his sheep.

But now I learn sight, sound and smells of the other dogs.

"Why do you growl at me?" I ask a small white dog. He stands aggressively. His tail does not wag and his fur has risen.

"I do not like you," is his reply.

"How can you dislike what you do not know?" I ask curiously.

"I do not like black dogs," he sniffs.

"But only my coat is black. We are both dogs," I say, but he does not listen.

"A black dog bit me. I hate black dogs."

"That is silly." I now try to make him listen.

24

"I just hate black dogs," he growls.

"Perhaps you received a bite because you growled," I answer. "You may have seemed angry."

Still he does not listen. I lie watching, ready for attack. I do not understand why he wishes me harm. But I will not fight. My eyes, nevertheless, follow his movements.

His master comes, moving jerkily towards me, swishing a stick at me. I remain. This patch of earth on which I lie is mine. I will remain until I decide to leave.

"Shoo! Shoo!" the man shouts. "You stupid dog. Go away! Go away!" He waves the stick above my head. He too is angry!

I remain.

"Come," he calls to his white dog. "You don't want that nasty black dog to bite you."

I feel sympathy for the dog. He has a foolish master. He is being taught prejudice by man. I learn by observing.

I see two dogs fight but they are ill-matched. A large Doberman spars with a brown dog who has been snapping at his heels. The Doberman, named Corporal, is slow to anger, but once he has been provoked, you should stand back. The other dog is small and insignificant. But I do not interfere. What is to be gained from fighting? What will they win? Nothing! They will lose only to themselves.

Corporal growls at me. I do not acknowledge. I am impartial. I am the onlooker. I only fight to defend myself or what is mine, the rest is foolishness.

Corporal's owner arrives in a fluster, unable to control this large dog who is now angrily starting to fight.

"Call your hound off," the man with the small dog snaps in a tone similar to that of his dog.

"He's just playing, that's all," Corporal's owner says, without conviction.

"If that's play I'm glad I'm not here when he's fighting," the man replies.

The dogs lose interest before the owners tire of their verbal abuse. Corporal ambles off. He has no speed, but he is flowing muscle.

"Come here, you stupid dog," the man snarls as he yanks at the small dog's collar. His temper is far worse than his dog's.

I wonder if the dog is bad-tempered because he lives with such a bad-tempered man? Man expects his animals to be what he is incapable of becoming – peaceful! Man is unjust, but we, the animals, will prove to be the survivors.

I reflect with sadness upon the order nature has decreed, for man has little or no order in his life. Our order is directness; we are not devious. We cannot lie for we know only truth. But man is a complexity, without loyalties to himself, his earth or its inhabitants.

I tangle not with other dogs. I am not foolish. I seek no distress. They are stronger than I, fiercer than I, so why challenge such as Corporal, who is proud. Let him feel king if this is his desire.

So, I watch many dogs bothered by needless orders, commands, instructions, directions, sadly from owners more confused than their dogs.

"Come here," goes the call.

"Sit down, you stupid fool."

"Stop that barking, will you?"

How I wish I could shout. "Teach us, please! We are anxious to please. We desperately seek your affection. But teach us what your contradicting orders mean."

I see poor, bewildered dogs, verbally abused, untrained, with large, sad, velvet-brown eyes searching the irate faces of their masters for some clue as to what is being said. They are accused, smacked and chastised. But who is the fool?

Man is kind. He pats us. But we need patience and understanding. Man is perverse, patting one second, hitting the next. Man lives so. It is from conflict that he gains his strength. He is cruel and I pity him.

He is the desolator through perversity, creating only

to destroy. In his cruelty he is the demolisher of life. My specie will survive long after man. Creator and destroyer – unsure, muddled and confused. I have the knowledge born from nature. I learn only from man about his world.

But the woods are mine. I run and run, feeling the breath breaking through my lungs, feeling the earth beneath my paws, the wind whispering in my fur with its morning greeting and, above, the trees sighing. Seth. Run! Run! For life is good and you are young.

A squirrel leaps high above from tree branch to tree branch, teasing me, and the birds sing me their secrets as I run by.

There is much to be thankful for on such a morn, but only I have time to see, to smell, and to hear.

Man hurries by, missing the trees in full bud, missing the sky above. He is forever rushing. Feet dash over the cinder paths, there are trains to catch so no time to waste in looking, seeing, hearing.

Feet drag through dust, scuffing with discontent. There is school to attend, shopping to be done. They see nothing; they hear nothing; they smell nothing of the day's dawning. To them it is like any other day. To me each day reminds me of the light I sought, and I give thanks as I run through these woods.

Now a large dog bounds towards me. I stop. I remain still. Slowly he sniffs, telling me he is a German sheepdog. He is powerful and I am wary.

He is Max. He is strong, but I am deft. Together we run through the woods. He tells me his master fears him. That I believe!

"Soon," Max says, as we stand waiting for our masters to catch up, "soon he will take me home. I am bored. I need more exercise to keep fit."

His master approaches, large stick in his hand.

"Now he is going to throw the stick and I am supposed to fetch it," Max sighs. "I think he enjoys the game."

"Max!" The stick is thrown and he obligingly goes after it.

I watch. I do not fetch sticks – yet.

"Seth. Come." I hear my master call.

I obey.

"Good dog." I receive a pat.

… and love.

Daily the brush goes over my coat and my tail is fanned out. I am much admired. My territory becomes the woods and the garden. Am I possessive? In the woods I see small woolly creatures yapping at me. They look like lambs, they should be lambs, but they smell strange. My inner reason, born and bred with instinct, tells me they are sheep-like. I know confusion as I attempt to round them up. Moving slowly, so slowly, round and round. No need to bark. I persist. They yap back at me. Do sheep yap? This I do not know.

"Seth." It is a command. "Leave the poodles alone."

I do not understand. They are white and woolly. What is a poodle?

"They are not sheep," the old rough-haired Collie says as she wanders leisurely through the woods.

"But they look like lambs," I reply.

"They are dogs like you and I."

"They have wool?"

"They are still dogs. You must learn."

"Funny dogs." I feel determined to have a final word. "What is your name?" I ask this Collie.

"Lassie," the old Collie replies. "My master is totally without imagination."

"I am Seth," I say. "Named after Adam. I am a son of this land!"

The Collie shakes her head. "Man is the son of the land; you are here to serve. Do not get over-confident, proud or big-headed," she tells me, gruffly. "Remember, you are fortunate. You are well groomed. You have a full belly.

Some do not. Work is the price you pay for the position you occupy on earth. You do not work. Others do long hours. Remember that, Seth."

"I know," I say. "I was bred in a dark shed. I will not forget. I know the darkness."

"Darkness and an empty belly," Lassie continues. "Many remain thus. Man discards what he does not need, what he does not like, what he loses interest in. Many wander soulfully searching, never to find. In the end to be exterminated."

I hear the seriousness and I ask, "What is that word?"

"Oh Seth," she sighs, "you have much to learn about man and his ways."

"Man does not believe animals should die without aid. Man believes he should choose our time. He pretends it is for our good. He is a great pretender – that is man."

I do not run, I walk, head and tail down, thinking. Can this be man? Will it happen to me?

"Run Seth, whilst you may," the trees whisper. The birds sing to me, "Death comes swiftly to us all; how it comes does not matter. It is life you must think about now, and how you can live it. Teach man, Seth. Teach man to become biddable."

*

I run through the woods. The wind is within my coat, the leaves are beneath my paws, the trees shade me from the all-seeing light, and I have found freedom.

I sense space and life. I smell its wonder.

"Seth! Seth!" the voice calls, breaking through my freedom. I stop. "Seth!" The voice is displeased.

The leash is placed on my collar. I know now that within all freedom there has to be a discipline. So I have learned. I have heard and I have obeyed.

Discipline suits man – sometimes.

… and trust.

The hillside is so steep! I climb with the master. I smell the sheep and know they are there, white dots on the lush verdant land. I know that I am known to them, as they are known to me.

I do not chase the sheep – I am a gatherer – so they do not run from the keeper of the sheep.

We lie now, the master and I, in the lushness of green mountain grass and the sun warms my coat. The flies buzz their song in my ears and my nose twitches at the scent of life.

I close my eyes and drift between reality and the dream of old. The shepherd is on the hill. High, high on

The wind is within my coat, the leaves are beneath my paws,
the trees shade me from the all-seeing light,
and I have found freedom.

the hill and there is no sound, just a stillness.

I am his, the sheepdog. I am he who must gather in his sheep.

"Seth!" I open my eyes. It is the master's voice and the dream vanishes as reality returns. We move, climbing higher and higher. The watchful mountains, chattering waterfalls, but there is no shepherd calling me to gather his sheep. Only in the distance, breaking through the peace, comes the vibrant voice of my master.

The day is ending, the mountain path trails below. Slowly panting, mud-clad, I descend back to the world of what is. The shepherd and the sheep are but a dream.

I am tired and the master calls again.

I move slowly, with grace, through the grass that murmurs in sympathy. I do not run. But neither do I crawl! The master waits; he is human and has frailties.

I walk to his boots. I sit and wait, for I smell his anger.

My master does not hit me. I am glad, for my bones are fragile. He *is* angry. Words I do not understand are poured over me. I absorb his irritation. My freedom is curtailed, but what is freedom? I walk at his heels without dejection. I accept his orders; there is no loss of dignity. We return from the land of the shepherd to the land of the master.

*

"Seth !"

I hear the voice, and lie as the young hands stroke me. They gently tickle my ears.

"You've been with the sheep." And there is laughter and fun in his voice.

I have learned to know those young hands that lay themselves on me. I give of myself in return.

"Seth."

I move quickly. It is the master, and I have the mud combed from my coat. I relax and sigh. The dark shed is my dream. I have become my name. I am Seth.

The early morning light comes through the trees. It is a long hot day of the summer of my life. There is a faint rustle in the garden as nature wakens to her day. I hear the scratching and scurrying of small feet on the roof of my kennel.

"Who is walking above me?" I ask as I slowly move from the comfort within to be greeted by the warmth of the sun. I stretch and smell the glory of this new day. "Good morning, Dee-o-jee."

I glance up and see the sharp penetrating eyes blinking at me. "Who are you who walks on my roof?"

"I am blackbird, Dee-o-jee," she chirps, picking up crumbs from my bowl.

35

"Why do you call me Dee-o-jee?" I yawn sleepily and move to lap up water that is tepid on my tongue.

"That is your name, Dee-o-jee." Blackbird hops on to my bowl, her beak points to the letters there.

"That's not my name." I lap more water.

"It says, Dee-Oh-Gee." Blackbird spells it out.

"It is not my name, that says, DOG!" I tell her. "That tells you I am a dog."

"Did you not know you are a dog?" Blackbird cocks her head to one side enquiringly.

"Of course I know I am a dog," I reply as I stretch out lazily in the sun.

"Does your master not know then?"

"Know what?" I say, for I feel impatient with this silly bird.

"That you are a dee-o-jee?"

"Of course my master knows that I am a dog." I yawn loudly.

"Well, if you know you are a dog, and your master knows you are a dog, why put it on your bowl? Does your master drink from the bowl?"

"No, the master does not drink from the bowl." I am tired of the questions.

"Does the master have *Master* written on his bowl then?"

"No, he does not have Master written on his bowl."
But now I see how ridiculous it is and nod in agreement.
"It is just another of the strange ways of humans and not
worthy of too much thought."

"So what does your master call you then?"

"I am called Seth," I reply, returning to the shade of
my kennel.

"Goodbye Dee-o-jee-Seth," she chirps as she flies off.

More noise on the top of my kennel. Now I hear the
fluttering and squabbling of the greedy starlings who
descend in aggressive force, demanding. They fight and
steal in their anxiety to get a share.

A small, cheeky robin hops in front of my doorway.
Winking, he picks up the crumbs their fighting and peck-
ing make.

"They are foolish." The sparrow gathers all he requires.
"They fight each other, so none of them get a fair share.
They are not united, so I benefit without working. I just sit
back and wait for the crumbs they so carelessly drop."

"Ah, you are wise, Robin," I answer. "Aggression is
the action of fools."

… and sadness.

Summer days! When the earth meditates with the sun, and

the stupidity of youth has blossomed into leaf. The summer is good to behold yet passes too soon.

"Come Seth!" I lie in the back seat of the car, hearing the familiar hum of wheels moving along the highway, and the steady drone of the mechanical horse, man's lazy way of covering ground, and I have become one of the carried.

Soon I hear the rhythm beneath give way to a different song as the sound of gravel and stones makes painful tunes on tyres. No clippety-clop, as metal hits flints, just the hiss of synthetic rubber slithering on stone. I am alert; my nose tells me, my eyes see, and my ears hear. I know they are near, I feel their presence ... and the forever smell of sheep. Sheep! Sheep!

*

In the goodness of the day I learn, feeling light from above, and a voice whispering, "Run, run, into the summer fields of life."

But it is not to be. I am leashed. We walk together, my master and I. He treads purposefully over the lustre-lacking grass, worn thin by so many boots and mechanical horses. I am by his side, smelling and knowing the earth beneath my feet as a friend.

"Heel!" It is an order. I pull and my collar tightens. I cannot argue with the chain round my neck. I obey. It is my wish. Boots come muddy and smelling of the sheep. They stop in front of me.

"No," says my master. "I am no farmer. We come to watch the sheepdog trials."

A hand pats me – a rough, working hand. It goes down over my ribcage; a hand well used to dogs and sheep.

"Aye, 'tis a fine dog you have. He should be working out there with the sheep." The hand leaves my coat. "I'd buy him from you, sir, give you a very fair price."

My ears stick up. I lie now without moving, fearful.

"No," my master laughs, his hand coming down to my head. "Seth is not for sale." The muddy boots move off.

I lie and wait, alert again. It is a strange scene. There are many dogs like me. And people, always and everywhere, people! And noise.

We walk, the master and I. I see and hear the sheep. They call out to me. If only they could learn sense and direction, they could round up the dogs. But in life some have to follow and others lead, that too I know.

A Collie, black on white, works them from pen to pen. He is an able dog, quiet, strong and intelligent. Here is skill. I sit. I watch. I learn. Words of praise for the dogs come without hesitation from the onlookers.

Sheep are swiftly and certainly gathered, moved with precision and the skill of a natural artist by dog in tune with man's command.

It is a sight of confidence, love and empathy, when dog and man are at one with each other, knowing and trusted as the gatherer of the sheep and his shepherd.

Is man turning obedience into money? Will greed become the prevailer? Cash and cups, rosettes and ribbons, praise and pain – winning and losing. Sheep and dogs. High, high on the hills, a moving pattern, black and white on chequered cloth, obeying. Being biddable!

I wish ... but no, I am content. I am Seth, the watcher.

And after they have performed to the enthusiastic crowd, the Collies return tired and weary. Some are well praised. Bowls of milk are placed before them and I see affinity between dog and man. Love and faith.

Then I see a dog, limping, with bleeding paws, gazing upwards with painful eyes, waiting for words that never come from a master indifferent to his needs. Should I envy these dogs of the hills? A word of love, a pat – the price is not excessive. Why are humans not always kind and fair? Tired dogs move to the tent, lapping at the sun-warmed water, whilst man quaffs his ale.

Then I see hands that lift dogs into waiting trucks. Here is gentleness and care.

"Aye, 'tis a fine dog you have. He should be working out there with the sheep."

All around, the sheep, the dust, the smell, cars with their engines roaring. Humans and yet more noise. I turn to see hard hands throw a dog into the boot of a car and I feel the darkness. I think of the dog lying there. I remember Lassie. "Some dogs work too hard and have nothing, others do little and have far too much."

I am confused by what is human.

I hear a faint noise nearby and slowly turn. A poor, pathetic, mud-clad Border Collie is being savagely berated by an irate master. I see the cowed body. I see the hand lash out, and hear the yelp of fear. My fur rises and I get up, but I do not move. I wait.

I see before me poor Beth, who dwelt with me so long ago in the shed, in the darkness, that friendly darkness, away from humankind.

"Beth! Beth!" I say as I move as near as my leash will allow.

Sad tired eyes look at me. I lick her. She smells of sheep, mud, dirt and fear. Her coat is clogged with mud and she wears a thick heavy chain round her scraggy neck. She is so very thin.

"Oh Beth!" I cry as I nuzzle her. "Why does your master treat you so unjustly?"

Her eyes are weary, dirt encrusted and tear-filled. She is too afraid to speak. Her eyes move constantly to her master's face, waiting patiently for his harsh words, his cruelty. She knows nothing else.

Strife, hunger and hurt are all Beth will ever know until she dies. Humans to her will always seem cruel, unjust and vicious.

I remember Beth in the shed – so shy, so trusting, so in need of love. Beth so gentle. Man so harsh. I think of the fat, over-fed dogs who walk in my woods, as I look at this poor hard-working Collie. Beneath her mangy coat lies loyalty, obedience and trust. Man creates terrible pain for its own sake. Some dogs have plenty; others, like Beth, have nothing.

Why is life so cruel?

I perceive that humans are also cruel to their own, uncaring of their fellow men, selfish of times. Humans, the despoilers of this beautiful land. Humans who have intelligence to create but who can only ultimately destroy. I do not understand. Except to reason that if humans can be so cruel to each other, how will they defend or protect those beneath them who merely serve?

I learn about injustice. Perhaps soon I will learn more about compassion.

… and pity.

I have seen him before, this tired dog. His eyes are dim, his coat matted and unclean. There is a thinness about him too, and he walks painfully, each step of his paw a seemingly agonising one. His master, also old, also unclean and ragged, walks hesitatingly beside the dog. He seems indifferent to the suffering and pain within the animal.

I see them today as I speed through the park, and stop.

"Are you in pain?" I ask this poor old dog.

"No," he sighs, lifting mournful eyes to me. "I am just so tired."

"Why does he walk you so much?" I ask.

"How else would we move?" he replies.

I cannot answer him. "But where do you walk to?"

"Nowhere. There is nowhere to walk."

"He makes you walk even though it is painful and you are going nowhere!" I sound indignant.

"My master is cold; he walks to keep warm," he answers me.

"You are so thin. Does he hurt you?"

His tired, red-rimmed eyes, watery and fast approaching blindness, look into mine. I see wisdom, understanding and pity. Those eyes, I know, have seen much. "My master," this old dog says, "is a good, kind man. He goes hungry to feed me. He goes without warmth so I have a rug on which to sleep."

I show surprise.

He recognises my reaction and says, "All men are not cruel." Slowly he gazes up and there is love and trust in his dim eyes.

Now I see the wrinkled features of the old man, who with a bony, shaky hand, leans down and pats the dog's head.

"Oh Sam!" The voice trembles and is full of anguish. "We are both so old and weary now. Do your paws hurt as much as my feet do? Are your eyes as dim as mine? Are you cold and hungry too? Do you remember, like me, long ago when it was not like this? We had food in our bellies, and warmth. We were of good cheer." He wipes a tear from his eyes. "I would surely be dead without you, my faithful friend." He shuffles on.

Sam turns to me. "My master has cured me when I was sick, carried me when I was weary, comforted me when I was lonely and been a friend when I was friendless. This old man rescued me from early death. He has given me all he can give – his love. If I die he will be alone."

"Come Sam," the old man is saying. He bends again and gently touches the dog.

"Seth," Sam turns, "do not judge too harshly. Do not condemn too quickly. Sight and sound and smell must be tempered with knowledge and understanding. I fear you still have much to learn."

I stand and watch the old man slowly move. I see Sam nuzzle into his hand. I do not know who is guiding and who is following. They are one.

I have learned the meaning of love.

*

Autumn

*"... and a stranger they will not follow,
but will flee from him."*

The summer has passed. Those long hot days of leisure and pleasure in tall grass, scampering across wet sands and being chased by the incoming tide have gone. Where did those sun-tipped carefree days of youth go? Those long youth-filled days that never seemed to have an end. Many springs and many summers, and I have accepted them without any thought that after summer comes the fall.

Now I learn that time, which in the spring was my careless friend, is with the shortening days fast becoming my enemy. Insidiously, autumn is creeping into our lives; shadows of its approach are in the air.

The birds are no longer tiptoeing on my kennel roof, but massing together on telephone wires to mutter of long journeys, far lands and a warmth to come. They are excited, fluttering and chattering.

Now I have memories. Young, firm hands have grown from boy to man in the space of a few summers in my life. Now he who was young can pick me up without effort. It is he who now at times takes me for a walk. We are companionable, but he is not my master.

He chases me and hugs me to his broad chest. Into my ears, innermost secrets have been poured, his face so close to mine, his heart thumping against my coat, tears dropping softly onto my face. I listen to his agony of lost loves, shattered dreams and hope that sometimes seems hard to find.

"Oh Seth!" Sometimes the voice would break. "You are my friend, you understand."

My presence comforts him. My silence embraces him. My tongue licks his wounds and for a brief moment, when time is unimportant, we have empathy, this young man and I.

But now another comforts him. She has long, golden hair and she is sleek and slim. Blood-red, claw like fingers dig into my fur in a pretence of love and affection. An unseen foot kicks spitefully at my belly. I make no protest. I move away from the offending presence.

Now I feel a faint chill of autumn casting its cloak around us all. I shiver at the quick cold as icy fingers steal through the house, and my breath mists into the morn.

I feel the unease of apprehension.

... and solitude.

There is the first glisten of frost on the ground. I lie quiet and alone in my kennel. I am warm on the straw. I reflect on my learning of humans and their ways, for I have survived. I have become biddable.

As I lie in the silence of my world, I think of sheep, but I now have to accept I am not of the sheep. I know only the shepherd of my dreams, but he has not bid me to come to him. Not he who is the shepherd of sheep, but he who is the shepherd of man.

"What are you waiting for?" Robin perches on my bowl and finishes off my breakfast.

"I am waiting to go for my morning walk," I reply. Patience with man is something I have learned and accepted.

"You wait a long time." Robin is cheeky.

"I have no time but his time," I answer this inquisitive bird. "He is my master."

"I have no master," Robin replies. "I was born free."

"Your freedom makes you hungry, so you feed from my breakfast, a breakfast my master provides for me," I tell the bird.

49

"But I am still free!" Robin tries to sing, but he is not successful.

"Freedom is but an illusion." I know this to be the truth. "You are responsible to your fledglings, when you have any," I say, cuttingly, "and you wait for crumbs to be thrown to you because the ground is too hard to dig for your own food." There is an angry flutter of wings.

"I go where I please," Robin insists. "You are chained."

"Yes, I am chained. Freedom is as much, or as little, as you are given. A chain is long or short. We are all chained. I am chained to protect myself from wandering and to reassure my master that I am here."

"I have no chains," Robin twitters. "No one could chain a bird."

"No," I nod my head wisely. "A bird is encaged for man's pleasure. No man could encage me. A cage I would not accept, but a chain binds me to my master."

"I am bound to no one," Robin insists.

"Everyone is bound to someone or something. You see my chains." I get up slowly and walk round to show the thin links of chain. "I could break the chain if I wished, but I choose not to do so; the choice is mine. Everyone has invisible chains, this I know. But I see my chains. It is the invisible chains that are usually stronger, and more binding. It is they that make you a prisoner."

"You talk foolishly, dog. I have no chains that are invisible. I am free." Robin pecks at more crumbs. "You cannot fly."

"No I cannot fly, but then, you cannot run. You can only fly for so long, then you need to rest. I can run and run. We can only do what we are designed to do. We cannot change ourselves and it is foolish to try. I am a dog, you are a bird. You cannot become me, I cannot become you. That is the way our creator intended us to serve. No one is free, not even my master."

"But he has no chains," Robin says scornfully.

"He is chained to me," I reply with certainty. "He cannot go out without seeing to my needs. He is responsible for me and to me. He is chained to me by that invisible chain. We are all bound to each other and that is the order of life."

"I think you are stupid." Robin cocks his head to one side as the sound of my master approaches.

Robin, who is free, is frightened and flies away. I, who am chained, am not afraid.

"Come Seth." The voice is firm but kind. He is a good man, this master.

Now I walk by his side. I am no longer chained. I am free, but I do not wish to run far. Freedom is a myth. Freedom comes with responsibility. Responsibility, that is my freedom. Why should I abuse it?

I am thankful for the good life I know. The boundaries of my life may seem limited to some, but I know my boundaries and I accept what is to be. By accepting I have widened my boundaries. Should I have disputed with my master, then I would have narrowed my boundaries – a lesson man could do well to learn, I think.

The woods are wide and high. There is good clean earth beneath my paw. I meet with Max, I meet with Lassie and we run together.

I see grey long fluffy tails that scamper up trees quickly. They jump from branch to branch overhead. Once I tried to climb, but I learned I cannot do so. Lassie tells me these delicate beautiful animals are squirrels. She advises me not to climb.

I have learned that accepting my limitation is wise. I must abide by what I can do, not what I wish to do. I lope away and pretend disinterest, and that annoys the squirrels more than my bark. But I do bark sometimes, a deep brown bark. I know I am intelligent, swift of paw and sure. I am responsible. Today I bark at the squirrels in the trees who sit and tease me. It is to let them know I have seen them.

I sniff and now chase the stick; it is a game for my master, and he loves it. Suddenly the quietness of the woods is shattered by the yapping of a small, insignificant dog.

"Why do you keep on barking and yapping?" I ask this small dog as he stands at the bottom of his garden overlooking the woods. His yapping is loud, so that with each attempt at being heard his whole body seems to lift off the ground.

"To let you know I am here," he replies.

"You make too much noise for no reason," I tell him quietly.

"I am small, people ignore me," he yaps back.

"Barking just irritates when there is no reason. What do they call you?"

"I am Jamie." He wags his small tail, and when he is not yapping he is a nice, friendly dog.

"Then, Jamie, do not bark all the time because there is no need; you are being silly."

"I like barking," Jamie snaps back. "I like being heard."

"It is because he is so small. He feels insignificant and that makes him lack confidence so he barks and barks." Lassie joins me. "Small often means noisy," she concludes.

We leave the silly little dog to his barking, and we run and talk together. The sun is low in the sky and the long shadows cast themselves around us. It is a cool, clear autumnal day, with the last remnants of summer hovering in the waiting air.

But it will not last. In the distance I hear my master approaching. His step is slower.

But now I only walk beside him. Somehow, the on-coming shadows make me wish to remain near him. This man has offered me a freedom and with his freedom has come trust; with trust has come love. I have no wish for a freedom that brings loneliness.

We walk together and the leaves have turned to copper petals. Like confetti, they fall, strewing the pathway, which in the final shaft of sunlight from the closing day, lights the way, gilded and glowing.

… and prison.

Autumn and I see them, and behold, it is a horrifying sight that animals such as I have not before witnessed.

Beautiful, sleek beasts are designed by nature for something other than to prowl around in a box with thick iron bars.

They arrived in the night, stealthily. Here, in my park, are tents and caravans and cages. I can only stand and gaze at the magnificence, the grace and the pathos, wondering about their captivity.

What purpose is there when animals pace a square? What is the reason? Human reason?

This man has offered me a freedom and with his freedom has come trust; with trust has come love.

The large cat with amber-coloured eyes looks out sadly through the slats of steel. I sense despair.

Nature must have created these animals for something other than this, I reason. I feel their degradation as if it were my own. I hear the pounding and shuffling as weary limbs try to stretch in matchbox spaces. I see dejection in spirits waiting for release from this living nightmare, which humans have created. I smell a waiting death. I meet misery, and I feel a deep shame within me as I take on myself man's ultimate in cruelty.

"Why are you caged so?" I ask hesitatingly.

The large creature stops aimlessly pounding round and round. Eyes full of frustration meet mine.

"We are animals for the circus and zoo. Man keeps us to perform for him."

"Perform?" I do not understand.

"We do silly tricks, little dog." There is bitterness and hate in his reply.

"Why?" I ask.

"I do not know."

"Was it always so – a cage for you?"

"I do not remember," he sighs.

"Are you happy?"

"What is happiness?" His voice is without emotion. "Soon, if I am lucky, I will die, and then I will be free."

"Are there many such creatures as you behind bars?" I am bewildered.

"Yes." His voice is now bleak. "Man has us for his amusement. I have seen much. "There is little left to hurt us, surprise us, or shock me, about the ways of humans."

"Tell me, tell me, please!"

"There are fish that swim round in jars of water. Beautiful, golden fish from shining countries where the water is pure and warm, now condemned to die in a cold glass jar.

"There are exotic birds, smuggled from their natural habitat, huddled in hampers; many to die to make gold for man.

"Tortoises from warm lands, transported to die in cold, frosty outhouses. Dolphins, friendly, fearless, lovers of life, waves and sea, captured by man to splash in pools, performing useless acts for clapping hands. Dying, lonely in despair.

"And seals, slaughtered in what man calls a cull – not a kill.

"Hunting, as man trains animals to kill not for food, not for protection, but for something he calls sport.

"Man uses animals for experiments, and some animals are killed for the ivory they bear, the coats they have, their head and their horns." He pauses and I see tears in his great amber eyes. "Endangered species, but who made them so?"

I see a huge creature such as I have not seen before. I have a twinge of fear as the large head and peculiar nose turn to me.

"Of what manner of animal is that?" I ask fearfully.

"An elephant! His tusks are ripped from him by ivory hunters, then he dies, slowly and sadly."

"Ivory!"

"White and bright to make beads and bracelets, Buddhas and bookends, crucifixes and crosses."

"I did not know," I say.

"Oh little dog, if we could take man and make him the endangered specie, then he would utilise his knowledge for good ... and love."

"But all humans are not so," I have to say.

"No, but their voices are weak and seldom heard. Protesting is not popular."

"Quite a circus you have here." It is the voice of my master.

"Aye, we do that." The voice is rough. "Bring the kids to see them perform." He bangs a stick against the bars of the cage. There is a snarl, a token of defiance.

I return home, sadly pondering on how little I know. How little I understand.

So autumn is for reflecting, remembering and assessing. The woods are stark; trees are shorn of their adornment. Autumn sifts through what has been, knowing what is to come is not as much as what has gone before. Nature prepares for the coming winter, preparation and revision.

*

Winter

*"I am the Good Shepherd ... the Good
Shepherd giveth his life for his sheep."*

Quietly they have gone: the spring, the summer
and the autumn. Winter has come.

Now I turn, and there is hurt in my limbs;
it is painful to run. The woods are bare and unfriendly,
the ground hard. It cuts into my paws. Today the master
and I walk together. There is a whimper at my tail. I see
a young pup wanting to run and play. He lies at my feet,
baring his soft, pink belly to my misting eyes. I sniff at him
and then give a low growl telling him to be off. I do not
wish to play, not today; it is too cold and I can no longer
run well.

The master too feels the new sharpness in the air. The
wind, no longer my friend, blows hard swift gasps across
my fur, making it rise with each breath.

And the trees that have watched me run and bound
through the too-short years, send down a mantle of leaves
in sympathy for my pain, a delicate carpet of brown and

gold and orange; a cape on the uncompromising earth for weary pads to tread.

I have chased the stick, chased the squirrels, now I can no longer run with breathless joy. I prefer to walk.

"Play with me," squeals the pup, who has much to learn. "Run and play."

"No." My voice is deep. "There is no purpose in running. That is for the young. It is winter, and I can no longer run with youth."

"You are getting old, Seth," the pup says in the callow voice of unsympathetic spring.

I sigh, remembering for a brief second how it used to be. "Yes, I am getting old." There is sadness within me.

The pup runs through the leaves and I watch and know there is envy behind my tears at his boundless energy and love of life.

My master arrives. His footsteps slowly crackle through the leaves. There is no spring in his walk on this cold winter morn.

Lassie and Max have gone. I know not where. One small dog told me Lassie's master had gone abroad and Lassie had gone to a new home.

Life is to be lived: joyously, sadly, happily, miserably. Death is but the epilogue – or perhaps the prologue.

And Max. I know nothing about poor Max, who grew old and forgetful, and slow. They say he wandered away and was killed by a car, but I do not know, except that I no longer see him in the woods.

Sometimes – just sometimes – I think I see Lassie and Max in the distance, running, running as they used to do. But I am slow, and when I finally reach the spot, they have gone and I can never catch them.

We are all shadows. Expendable. That I have learned from humans. It still puzzles me. Death is always at hand, yet man is not content with such knowledge for he pursues death with relentless determination, seeking it out as a hunter would a quarry.

Now it is late, and I tire as I walk. We are both slow, the master and I.

Winter, the artful creeping finger of time, chills our bones.

My master stops, and I hear a strange voice. A strange hand tentatively pats my head. I smell a strange old smell.

"Nice dog, well taught."

I hear my master laugh. "Yes, he is a good dog, extremely intelligent. Gets his own way through sheer persistence – dogged determination!" He leans down and strokes my nose.

"We've had some good times together, Seth and I." The master's voice is sad, and I know that, like me, he misses the long days on the moors, misty mornings when he could stride forth throwing the stick for me. Then I would run through the bracken and the streams, always with the smell of life in my nostrils, the sweet awakening of my limbs, and the running.

"Now Seth is old like me."

He moves away. I stand up and there is an ache in my back limbs. I stagger a little as I try to keep up. He turns. "Come on Seth!" There is impatience in his voice.

I try to tell him that I feel pain, but he has moved away and I am left to stagger.

"You are not running today?" the cheeky poodle snaps at me, but I cannot reply for the pain.

"Seth!" My master stops. "What's the matter, old chap?" He pats my head. "Come on, time we both went home."

Side by side, and slowly, we walk together through the oncoming dusk of life.

In the warmth of the kennel I fall asleep, fearing the pain and dreaming of meadows and mountains.

I have great difficulty in walking. The vet runs his hands expertly over my limbs. I utter a faint murmur, to tell him that I hurt.

"All right old boy." He speaks to me with understanding as he leaves me standing on the bench. He knows I will not move.

There is a sharp penetrating pain as the needle jags. I do not yelp. The pain is nothing to the agony I have suffered. Maybe I should thank man for the relief it gives me.

"That'll help you. You're getting old." The vet turns to my master. "Don't let him do too much. You know he'll never give in, but his legs are not as young as they used to be. He has to take it easy from now on."

I am picked up and lifted from the examination table. The hands are strong and firm and confident round my belly; the hands of he who was young with me. He does not spend much time with me now for another has entered his life. But she, unlike the other, is kindly towards me. I sense her knowledge and love of dogs as she strokes my head with affection.

And occasionally, when she has gone, he will kneel down and hug me close as he did all those summers ago. His voice will whisper in my ear, "Do you approve of her, Seth?" And I will lick his hand so he knows that I do. I am glad he does not forget me.

But the days are shorter now, drawing to a close as night comes in so swiftly. I try to recapture an enthusiasm walking, but I cannot. No sticks to chase. No squirrels. No friends.

I am fussed over. Pills ease my pain. I am rubbed down with a hot warm towel when it rains. My coat is groomed and I am kept clean. Each morning I am given an egg in warm milk.

I am contented. I accept that this is winter, and I reflect that my other seasons were good.

… and grief.

There is something wrong. I sense it. The house is quiet. There is a stillness such as I have not felt before. It is like the darkness from my past, a chill of the unknown.

I hear my master. He speaks to me softly from his bed. He lies there now all day, resting quietly in the dusk-filled room. I remain still. I lie by the side of his bed, where they let me stay.

I raise my weary eyes and lick his hand as it comes and unsteadily scratches my ear.

"Oh Seth!" His voice is faint. "Do you remember all those days we had together? I wonder, where have all those years gone?"

I too lie sighing, thinking of him striding through the grass over the hills, calling me to heel so that I would not chase the sheep.

Unconsciously I give a faint whimper at the memory of how it used to be. I nuzzle his hand and I know he is sad like me. Our thoughts bind us together. This man has been my master for so long. Such love and trust exists. My limbs ache, but I manage to sit up and move my nose beneath the bedcovers.

"You are a good dog, Seth," he says. "The best dog a man could wish for."

Together we join in memories, both of us climbing the hills, hearing the slush of boots on mud, as he strides confidently forward whilst I am always nearby.

"We've been some places you and I," he murmurs. "You're a well-travelled dog, Seth." He rubs my nose and my eyes water.

I can still hear it and feel it all: the sun on my fur; the sweat dripping from my tongue; the gentle rain and the coolness of water on my paws. And sheep – I can still smell them sometimes as I dream of those good old days.

I remain at the side of the bed. The hand continues to stroke my head. I close my eyes. I am travelling with him in his car. The soft breeze from the sunroof cools me. He is talking and I am happy.

The journey to the sea. The journeys to the towns. Hotels I have stayed in, where I have been showered, a gentle stream of rain cleansing my dusty coat. Trains in the highlands. So much together, for so long. I dream of what has been. For what is to come is no dream.

Suddenly the room is silent and a darkness has crept in unnoticed. I move a stiff limb. I feel an unknown presence, but I am not concerned for I recognise the presence as a friend.

I move to lick the master's hand reassuringly. It is strangely cold to my touch. I wait for the fingers to move, but they are motionless in this dark room.

With an insight that has survived from an existence I know not where, I accept, acknowledging the presence. It is He, the shepherd gathering in the sheep. I am to realise later that the winter of my life is almost over.

... and rest.

No longer does his voice call me. He is lying cold and calm in wood. There is much crying. I feel the great overwhelming sadness of a time that has gone. It cannot return.

He came into my life so long ago, lifting me from darkness. Has he too left his darkness to find the light?

"He is biddable." The voice whispers in my ear, ghosts from the past chasing through my dreams. My ears prick up, and for one brief, glorious moment I am young again, chasing the stick, waiting for him to tickle my belly.

The woods are full of spirits of what has been. Sounds and smells.

I slip into the bedroom and lie as I did, by his bed, pretending that he is stroking my head, whispering, "good dog." But the whisper is only the wind mocking me.

It is the young hands that bore me that day from the shed that now try to comfort me. But there is little they can do to erase the memory of he who was my master.

"He is a one-man dog, is Seth," he says, stroking me with the hands of a man. But they are not *his* hands. "What shall we do with you?"

I know the answer, and so do they, although they have not acknowledged it. My days are short. There is a brief spell between walking and sleeping. The rest is memory.

The house is quiet. He used to fill each room with his presence. Now there is void. His scent is everywhere about me.

I slip into the bedroom and lie as I did, by his bed, pretending that he is stroking my head, whispering, "good dog." But the whisper is only the wind mocking me.

The woods are barren. Branches straggle out-stretched fingers pointing to the leaden sky. Leaves curl up in anger at the cruel frost. Sometimes a down of snow flits over my coat, and I recall my first encounter with the friendly flakes.

I am slow of pace, my legs ache. My eyes are tired. My ears do not hear as they should, and my heart is heavy with loss.

I remember and it is all grief. Oh, where is Clyde? I think of the shed. Beth, poor sad lonely Beth. Where have all those dogs from the shed gone? Spirits of the nights, smells, sights and sounds.

I have learned the pain of memory.

"Perhaps we should put him down."

There is sadness in the voice.

"He is dying of a broken heart. He misses the master."
It is she who strokes my ears.

So many voices planning the short time I have left. But what do they know?

I limp to the corner of the room and lie down. I am so tired.

Far away, I hear the voice calling.

"Seth! Seth! Come on, run! Run!"

And it is time.

I sigh and close my eyes.

*

The Longest Journey

Out of life comes death,
and out of death comes life.
Out of the young, the old.
Out of the old, the young.
The stream of creation
and dissolution never stops.

"Oh Seth!" It is the son of my master. "I held you when you were a pup; you have been a part of my life for so long. I will miss you. Oh Seth, dear friend, forgive me."

I feel a strange hand over my body. I hear a strange voice. I feel the twinge of a needle. Pain! It is but a dream. All is now beyond my worldly thought.

The woods stretch alive in spring celebration green. The sky is airbrushed blue. The sun kisses me and the trees wave timorously.

My master is striding with purpose in the distance, and in the shadows I see Lassie and Max.

I have learned to say goodbye to the illusion of life. For I see the mirror image of the tired old Border Collie who lies so still. I see the firm hands of he who was young with

71

me. They stroke the coat. I feel no touch. I hear no sound. A tear is shed but I feel no sadness.

I am Seth, born of the earth, no longer that aged dog with creaky joints. I am without fear, as I am enveloped in a warm friendly darkness that eases over me like a blanket of the night.

My way lies ahead and I am bidden by an invisible shepherd. Now I must learn about the illusion of the hereafter.

I see the dog. He walks beside me. He is small and gentle.

"Who are you?" I ask.

He is friendly and wags his stumpy tail. "I am called Death."

But I know no fear for I have not met death before. We walk together and I see the way ahead – a long tunnel. As I enter, Death disappears. I am wrapped in darkness; it has been my friend before.

The ground beneath my pads is familiar. The sound ahead is known. I smell the way of the sheep and I know the shepherd waits. Now I seek truth and enlightenment.

… tomorrow was yesterday.

I travel along the narrow tunnel. There is no day and no night, all is sepia and soundless. I know no time. I am drawn forward. I feel no hunger. I feel no thirst. I know no weariness.

Now from the gloom I see a myriad of lights. They dance and in their glow the tunnel is no more. My limbs are overcome with sudden fatigue. My tongue is dry and my stomach feels empty. I watch a lascivious flame creep over the lights, bright orange, yellow, red and gold. There is a strangeness and I know there is heat and burning and crackling flames devouring.

I see a door. It opens before me. There is a dish of food, a bowl of water and the glow of warmth.

A voice from the shadows whispers, "Come in Seth."

The hair on my spine rises, for the words are his, but the voice is strange. With the instinct of time, I remain still and crouch on the floor.

The tunnel has become a wild and depraved place. I hear terrifying snarls, as if there is a great torment. Anger. Fear. Despair. The door has closed and I see the beast as it approaches me. It is such as I have not met before.

Biddable, I remain watchful.

Biddable, I am cautious.

Biddable, for I see no aggression.

The beast seeks no peace. By flame he is outlined. Smooth coat like polished ebony, bleak and black. His collar thickly glints with bright red stones like droplets of blood. His eyes are blazing amber, his ears pointed, his muzzle ferocious. White fangs warn me of his potential. His snarl is mighty.

Thunder claps above my head, wind seers viciously through my coat. Dust bites into my eyes and chokes in my throat. I cannot bark. I cannot retreat. My way is only forward.

"There is food, there is water. There is your master." The beast stands and I feel the power he emanates.

"My way lies forward," I reply, for I do not trust this hound.

"You are a fool. Why travel on where the way is hard, when you can rest here and serve as I do?"

"Who are you?"

"I am the hound of hell. I can show you a life such as you have never had with man. You must just serve my master."

"I know of no hound of hell," I tell him, "and I have but one master."

"My master is the most powerful. He is the Devil."

"I know of no Devil."

"Man gives him many names: Lucifer, Satan, Demon, Beezelbub," the beast growls.

"But what does he do, this Devil?" I ask.

"He rules the kingdom below." The beast bids me to follow.

I smell the sulphur, I see the flames and the large gaping crater mouth. It is a place of fire and black desolation. There is moaning and wailing and creatures with arrow-shaped tails and blood-skin run with tridents in paw-like hands. And Devil-dogs roam at will.

"In this land, man and beast get whatever they desire," the beast tells me. "There is abundant food and drink. Come Seth, and join us." His tail swishes back and forth, but I feel no friendship for this dog.

"What must I do?"

"You must take the Devil for your master."

"I have a master; I need no other."

"You are a fool," he snarls.

"But who would create such as the Devil and this horrible land?"

"Man has created it. Watch and I will show you the mind of man." He throws back his head and howls.

I stare before me and see with horror the leopard with the feet of a bear and the mouth of a lion.

"What is that?" I back away as I see the cock-snake."

"A basilisk. It kills with a single glance."

I turn and see a beast with seven heads and then, through the monstrous mist, I see the red cock regurgitating a green snake regurgitating a black hog.

"It is horrible." I move away.

75

"They are servants of my master. They represent greed, hatred and delusion, the qualities in man that poison his life."

The stench of the place fills my nostrils. I want to run, far away, back to the fresh cleansing grass, back to the light and the sweet smell of goodness. I rise and move away and as I do I see pounding towards me an apparition with its human head, lion's body and scorpion tail. I crouch back on this rim of hell.

"Oh, what is such a creature?"

"A Manticore, and over there …" Devil dog nods to the winged serpent with the second head on a tail-tip. "That is an Amphisbeana, and there is the Blemye, and over there the she-beast Chimera."

I bark now with pent-up fear at this vile, fire-breathing horror with the head and body of a lion, with a goat's head sticking out of its back and the hissing tail of a serpent. I wish to see no more of this intense hatred and misery, for there is nothing that is not vile and putrid.

"Why are there such creatures?" I ask.

"They have been created by the minds of humans. Vicious thoughts of war and hatred, perversions and hell have created this. Thoughts that were written into space to become immortal."

I wish only to move from this place. Now a mist clouds out the scene and when it parts, there are my woods again with long, leafy branches beckoning to me. I wish to run, but caution bids me wait. Then the leaves part and I see the serpent.

"My master!" Devil dog sighs.

"A serpent!"

"Man got it all wrong really, for what should have been good became bad. Man thinks of the Devil as a serpent, another illusion I fear."

The serpent has gone and my ears flatten against my head as I see emerging from the smoke a frightening shadow, half man, half goat.

"That's him again," Devil dog says wearily.

"Are you afraid of him?"

"I can only fear what man will create into the scene," he replies.

Now I feel pity for him.

"I am tired of being a Devil-dog," he says. "Tempting people into hell, for that is my purpose. It instils fear into humans, for out of fear comes goodness. It is fear of all this, that makes humans good, you see."

"And does it?" I ask.

He cannot reply for a voice calls, "Satanic, come."

Then thunder roars and lightning fragments across the growing storm clouds, scattering the darkness. The light penetrates and the scene crumbles into dust. I am back in the tunnel and the light is before me. I will not deviate from this journey. Now I have recognised a fear of the unknown in humans. It is called evil.

The lightning, bright and clean, is more powerful than the flames of hell. I am no longer hungry. I am no longer thirsty. I am no longer alone.

I am contented now to wait.

I sense another dog moving slowly towards me, but I sense this is no Devil-dog.

"Who are you?" I ask cautiously.

"I am Bernard," the growl reassures me.

I see the form of a large dog with a kindly, good-humoured face. He has a rough coat of brown and white. There is a large cylinder hanging round his neck.

"I am Seth."

"We have been expecting you."

"You knew I was coming?" I am surprised.

"Of course. Not the exact date, for man is always un-predictable. Conscience stricken at the final moment."

"I do not understand?"

"Well, whether he should or should not."

"Should or should not do what?" I ask.

"Exterminate you, of course." There is surprise in his voice. "Surely you did not think you had come here in your own time?"

78

I should feel sadness that he whom I trusted had disposed of me thus, but I cannot. I know it was done in kindness.

"What is that around your neck?" I ask.

"A barrel."

"Why do you carry a barrel round your neck?"

"To rescue men from the snowy wastes." He gives me a pitying look.

"What is in the barrel?"

"Brandy."

"But there are no snowy wastes in which you can rescue men here?" I am confused.

"It is man's illusion, and my purpose," Bernard replies as he prepares to move away.

I follow and my paws suddenly touch the crisp coldness. He leads on, his barrel making a track in the illusion of snow.

"What is hell?" I ask when we eventually stop to rest.

"Hell is an illusion made to make men feel they rise to heaven for goodness and fall into hell for badness. It is a device from the mind of humans to make them obey the rules of their Gods."

"What rules?"

"Rules not to kill, be envious, or greedy."

"But man is all of these things," I say.

Bernard looks at me with eyes full of pity. "Of course he is. They all interpret the books in their own way."

"The books?"

"There are rule books. Each gives the word of God and the followers of each book thinks theirs is the right way, and that causes war, conflict, and greed."

"Do they not see that?"

"They do not see the message, only the rules." Bernard shakes his head.

"What is the message?" I ask.

"The message is love. But it is too simple for the humans to understand. For our Creator is without sin, so how could he have created sin? Sin is in the minds of men."

We sit in a light that is neither day nor night and I think about what Bernard has said.

I wake and the darkness is now with me and then I hear noise.

"What is that?" I ask.

"Terror." I hear a sad tired voice, but I cannot see to whom it belongs. "It is the hunting dogs chasing the fox. It is cocks fighting each other to the death. It is the badger being baited. It is the fish being speared. It is the birds being shot."

There is sadness, anguish, hurt and humiliation. I feel it as if they were my own – the perpetual cry of creatures who cannot escape.

I lay my head on my paws, for I know the beginning of sorrow now.

"Do not cry, Seth." The voice is deep. "For if you listen you can also hear the cries of humans."

The noise is now horrendous. "What is that I hear?" I ask.

"It is abortion, war and murder," the voice says.

... the dawn.
The self is lesser than the least;
greater than the greatest.

"Come Seth. It is now time!"

I shiver on the straw and see the sudden swift arrow of light speeding across the shed. I remain quiet for I know there are others such as I waiting.

And they come. Shep, who was so boisterous, is now submissive and quiet. Blackie, once so timid, snaps with aggression. Jake, so confident and sure, so sleek and fat. And Beth, so gentle, lies cowed in a corner.

We are together again, world stamped.

"What are we doing here?" Jake snaps.

81

From the gloom emerges Clyde. "We are here to learn," he says gruffly.

"Who is going to teach us?" Jake asks. "Not you, for you know nothing."

"I will learn," I say. "I have seen hell."

"Ah, Baby Ben, who was so biddable," Clyde says, reminding me of how I was then known.

"Boot-licker!" Blackie snarls at me.

"Better be a live boot-licker than a dead dog," Shep replies, and as he stumbles to his legs I see the scars and scabs and the dried blood on his mud-caked coat.

"Oh, what happened?" I ask.

"I was thrown from a car. They were drunk. They didn't want me any more, for I was old." His eyes are sad, reflecting the hurt within.

"So what is this place?" Jake asks as he swaggers round.

"This place is the *limbo-land*; the station on the way for thought and recollection. It is time for choice," Clyde says seriously.

"I will be a Devil dog," Blackie snaps. "I would make a good Devil-dog."

"You cannot be a good Devil-dog," Clyde replies angrily. "You can only be a bad Devil-dog. Think before you speak."

"Devil-dogs eat and drink well," Blackie argues.

"You must not become a Devil-dog," I say. "Tell us why you have become so aggressive?"

"There is no place for timidity, for the meek are cuffed and kicked. I was taught this; it is my defence." He bares his fang teeth. "I was bought by man and taught to be vicious. I was named Warrior."

"Warrior? What sort of a name is that?" Clyde sighs wearily. "Aggression only breeds aggression. We are here to learn again."

"What must we learn now?" I ask Clyde.

"Ah, Baby Ben, how named they you?" His eyes are kindly.

"I was named Seth."

"It is a goodly name, for you learned to become bid-dable and now you must learn compassion for humans, for you are in this shed to learn love. Through love we can put aside hurt, pain and conflict."

"I cannot forget pain." The eyes of the small dog are large pools of hopelessness. "They took me from the farm and abandoned me. I was lost, cold, and hungry and no one took me in. I was called Toss, and I was good with the sheep."

"All humans are not so," Clyde replies as he turns towards Beth, who remains huddled and shivering, her coat so shaggy, her eyes liquid pools of fear. I move across and lick her matted coat and then I feel the chain that has dug so deeply into her scraggy neck.

"Beth! What happened?"

She is too weak to lift her head and can only utter a pitiful whimper.

"She carries a chain," I say.

"We all carry chains, Beth will be free from hers …"

"How will she be free?" I ask impatiently.

But Clyde will not answer.

"I was well cared for," Jake boasts.

"You are too fat; that was no kindness," Clyde says dismissively, and turns again to me. "Seth, what have you learned from humans?"

"I remember the light from the shed, and he who was my master. I was not beaten. I was fed on good food. From man I learned of his good deeds. Kindly hands made me well, comforted and loved me. From man I learned caution and kindness but never fear." I say it all slowly.

"You have learned well, Seth. Will you now go forward?" Clyde asks.

The door of the shed swings open. Ahead there is a stony road. There is only white bright light, and the road is treeless.

"Let us stay, we are safe here." Shep curls up on the floor.

"The choice is yours, but once you make it there is no turning back. Think before you decide to go forward," Clyde says gravely.

"I will go." Jason has risen; he moves gracelessly towards the door.

"Beth, come!" I nuzzle at her until she slowly gets onto her thin, shaky legs, but the weight from the chain seems to drag her down. She cannot respond and I look to the others for help, but they are too busy thinking of themselves. "Come Beth." I pick up the trailing chain in my mouth. I feel the weight, but I cannot leave her, for she has suffered enough.

The chain that now binds me to Beth goes taut and she is forced to move. It is slow and painful, but it is forward to the light.

"Are you coming?" I ask Clyde, who has not moved.

He shakes his head. "I have to wait awhile, to give Blackie a chance to return from hell."

"But you told us there was no returning."

"There is always a small trap door out of Hell. It is very hard to find, but once you open it, then the destination of Hope is clearly marked."

"And Shep?" I look across to where he is sleeping.

The chain that now binds me to Beth goes taut and she is forced to move. It is slow and painful, but it is forward to the light.

"He is too tired to decide now. You go, for the darkness will return and the shed will close shortly."

"Clyde, will I see you again?" I ask

"I do not know, but be of good heart."

So Beth and I move from the shed. The rays dance to welcome us, and the road lies in front.

... the way ahead

Jason has long gone ahead of us. Beth is now tiring from the weight of the chain. Our journey is slow and the darkness has started to chase the light, so the streaky sky is now without sun. But I feel no cold. There is light, a flickering yellow and gold, edged with black lace.

But there is a nothingness. No fields, no trees, just expanse. Then a thin mist slowly covers the path. I sense the unknown and stop. My nose twitches for I recognise the scent. It is Bernard lumbering towards us.

"Where are we?" I ask as we crouch, now on a small plateau.

"This is the land of foolish fantasy," he replies.

The mist parts like a stage curtain. I hear Beth whimper and we huddle together, for we see a creature with the body of a serpent, the legs and claws of a bird, the head of a camel, the ears of a cow, the horns of a deer, the eyes of a rabbit, and teeth of a carnivore. The body is scaled with ridges and from the nostrils there comes smoke. But there is no aggression in this strangely composed animal, and I venture forth, alert and mindful.

"I am named Dragon," is the reply in answer to my question. "I am purposeful. I was once said to be killed by St George. I live in children's books. I am on flags and I live in the land of fantasy and myth. I breathe out clouds of rain or fire. I am found in the sky or the ocean or land. I am multi-purpose as well as being multi-coloured. I am red for the land, green for the ocean, yellow for the Gods. I am legend and all the forces of nature. I am man's unknown, his secret fear. I am what is; I am what is not. I dwell in the caverns of the mind, and coil in the fathomless deep of unconscious thought. I race through the sky when the storm brews. My claws scratch the heavens and lightning flashes. My voice is thunder, and my breath the red sky of dawn. I wash my mane in the whirlpool of man's desire. I am the emblem of emperors. I am real, as old as the mind of men and as young as the birth of a star. I am the Universe!"

"I like you." Beth has crawled slowly forward.

"Who bound your neck with a chain?" Dragon asks and I hear the approaching voice of thunder across the sky.

"My master," Beth replies.

The sky darkens and a flame of scarlet flashes. From the dragon's nostrils comes fire and the heat scorches the plateau. We do not move. There is a sudden burst of flame, and the chain around Beth's neck falls away.

The storm clouds disappear and Beth shakes herself as Dragon disappears back into the minds of men.

"You must go, for the journey is long," Bernard says.

Slowly we follow and we know not whence. Beth is weak and tired, but we cannot stop and rest for there is no shelter, just this never-ending road. Then suddenly, in the distance, I hear the steady pounding of hooves on earth, drawing nearer and nearer.

The horse is white. Magnificent. Proud.

The mane flies but there is no wind; the coat glistens, but there is no sun.

"Behold, I am Pegasus." His neck arches and his hoof paws the unyielding earth.

I sense this is no ordinary horse and then I see the furled wings by his side. I bark, for I am startled and a little afraid.

"I am a fable from the gods of time. Perseus slew the Gorgon Medusa, and from her blood I was conceived. Bellerophon rode on my back, attempting to reach Heaven. I am a constellation. I fly round the heavens. I am the star in the night. I am man's thoughts on wings."

With grace he slowly unfurls his great white wings. Beth moves forward, dragging one bleeding paw in front of the other.

Another white beast appears. I sense a strange beauty in the bodily attributes of a horse, but with the beard and cloven hooves of a goat. It has a single horn and the glow of light makes the whiteness of the coat gleam with iridescent purity.

"The unicorn!" There is a hushed reverence in Bernard's voice. "It is the symbol of purity. The horn is the magic of enlightenment." Bernard lies down.

The beast, though strange, looks gracious.

"Where are you from?" I ask.

"I do not know from whence I came. I am depicted in art as being hunted. I am a very common heraldic beast. It is said I can only be caught by a virgin, for I am purity."

I nod and then yawn, for I am tired and want only to sleep.

"It is all to do with good and bad," Bernard is saying knowingly. "Man makes evil black because he is too short-sighted to see, and purity white because he thinks he can see."

"Man is cruel," Beth whispers in a sad, despairing way and as she moves her head I see the scrawny, chain-scarred neck.

"No, misguided," I say, for I have not suffered so.

The sky turns deep red. The dragon appears and the darkness is blown away, but I remember no night.

Pegasus is snorting and his wings are outstretched.

"Climb on my back," he orders. "I will lighten your journey."

He folds his wings now and then kneels down.

"Goodbye," Bernard says. "I must go."

The unicorn stands silent and watchful as Beth and I climb onto the broad back of Pegasus. Then the great wings open and we are airborne.

I hear a voice from afar. I lie and forget fatigue.

This is the border of fantasy." Pegasus sets us down.

Beth and I stand and watch as he flies away high into the returning night sky, and then there are only stars glistening above. It is neither dark nor light, neither warm nor cold.

"Where will our journey end?" Beth asks.

"I do not know," I reply. "I think we are in the realms of man's imagination."

"Will we escape?"

"I do not know."

The road is hard beneath our paws. Our pads are torn and bleeding and we limp slowly forward. My coat is no longer silky and soft, but dusty and tangled.

Now there is nothingness, with a glimpse of memory, for as we walk all my dog-filled days are with me. Then I see a figure striding ahead of us. As Beth slinks behind me the man stops. He is menacing.

"You stupid cur," his voice is rough. His hands hold a thick, knotted piece of rope. He wields it viciously, so it slices through the air.

"You stupid, useless cur." His face becomes red with anger as he attempts to lash at Beth.

She cringes, her eyes beseeching, understanding from this man. I see his boot in the soft belly and I hear her yelp of anguish. I growl and move forward.

I feel the pain of the rope, a pain such as I have never felt. I feel an anger such as I have never known. I bare my fangs. I see his arm raised and wait for the blow for I cannot attack.

Then he falls and moans before us. His face is no longer red, his voice is no longer angry. He tugs as his collar. Beth moves forward. He is in pain, but without anger. His viciousness has gone and I see only fear in his eyes. He suffers.

Beth stands by his side, her brown eyes are compassionate now. Her tongue licks his forehead. His own eyes meet hers and then turn away, for he is ashamed. He raises his hand to caress or cuff. Instinctively, Beth moves away.

"I cannot leave him," she says. "He is my master."

"He has beaten you?"

"Yes!"

"He may beat you again," I say.

"But he is my master."

Darkness spreads her cloak and Beth sleeps. I remain awake. The dragon breathes out and the dawn is brightly gold. The master is gone. He is no longer in Beth's vision. Her pain had healed through compassion and love.

… back to the future.

The man is sitting by the side of the road on a small white stool. He does not look up as we approach. He is intent on making marks on paper with a pen.

His clothes are not such as my master would have worn. His boots are scuffed and worn, and I see his socks are of odd colours: one is yellow and the other is red. His trousers are of green cord, and his shirt is bright red.

We move nearer.

"Good dogs!" Now he glances at us, and I see his round, kindly face, with sparkling blue eyes and a mouth that smiles.

He holds his hands out to me and I know I have no reason to fear. His fingers are gentle on my coat and I recognise the touch of a man who knows animals.

"Come," he whispers softly to Beth, who cowers, her eyes fearful as she waits for the hands to strike her. Then slowly she wriggles forward on her belly.

"Do not be afraid." His hand is on her head. His fingers stroke her ears, and she waits for the blow, for kindness she has never experienced.

"You are so weary, and your coat so ill-kempt." There is sympathy in his voice. "I will help you."

He bends down and feels her neck, seeing the scars of the chain. I see a deep furrow on his brow. Then he reaches up to his ear and I see him take a pencil. He smiles, and a thin shaft of sunlight appears; the dark clouds disappear.

"Who are you?" I ask.

He laughs, and it is light and bright, like a flowing stream over pebbles.

"I am the rainbow dreamer," he replies. "I will draw you a dream."

He looks at me for a while and then I watch and see his pencil skim over the paper. I see the sky turn blue, and then I smell the green of the grass. I watch, and there are my woods, the birds singing, and there is a stream gurgling before me.

The man has gone, and it is as if he had never been, except for the dream around us.

We walk slowly to the stream. It is there. We drink from the water and then plunge in and the droplets welcome us and remove our dust.

We clamber to the banks. A wind dries us and the trees beckon us. The branches clap their hands as we run. Run! Run!

The leaves make a mantle for our paws. The birds are singing and there is joy. Beth is with me. Her eyes are bright and her coat is clean. We are one with the woods as we move through the patterns of light and shade.

Many dogs are joining us and I know them all. There is Lassie, and Max. We are chasing the stick and somewhere ahead just out of my sight is the master.

I am running towards him. Beth is with me.

We are young again. I am Seth, biddable and ready to learn.

The earth, our planet, had to be created for a purpose and the purpose had to be life, otherwise why are we here?

I am Dog. I am out of the womb. Out of the darkness, and the beautiful Earth is open to my eyes. I am cowed by its hugeness. I am enthralled by its splendour.

I have been given sight to see the clouds chasing the sun in an airbrushed sky, the stars winking, the moon smiling and the earth's life.

I have been given hearing to listen to the sound of rain, the swirl of leaves, the song of a bird.

I have smell to know the grasses, the blossom and the flowers of life.

I have touch to feel the cold snow beneath a paw, the soft lushness of grass and the warmth of sun-baked soil.

I have been called biddable for I am patient with man's stupidity.

I have been given life to learn.

I was born in a dark shed and bred by a shepherd to be a keeper of his sheep. I am a Border Collie. I have no name except that which is on my chipped bowl and I have been named by the robin who drank the tepid water with me.

I do not mind for what I am called does not matter; it isn't worth getting upset about. I am peaceful. I am biddable. I am intelligent. My home is the Earth and my shelter is a kennel.

I am content for there is nothing to be discontented about. The birds are my friends and they sing to me as the dawn crashes through the darkness and the sky breaks into its morning smile. I listen, for I have all the time in the world.

There are so many birds in coloured coats who sing, and I know them all by their song. Some have a very shrill song, and some are all warble. Some are low and some high and some are soft, and some are very much out of tune. But they all have a place and a purpose.

Then comes the gentle coo of the wood pigeons as they commune to the day, and overhead a kestrel hovers, head motionless whilst it searches for prey. I feel a sadness knowing that somewhere in the field is a scared little mouse who has strayed too far from his nest, and I hope it will miss the kestrel's beak.

In the distance there is a small woodland. The breeze is teasing the trees so they dance and sway as if to an unseen band and I know the boy will be coming soon.

He is young, like me, with bright fair hair that shines in the sun and blue eyes. The wind is breezing through my coat; the sun is shining all around.

I gaze up at Him and on the branches there is the beginnings of new.

I am reborn.

The End

I am Seth - I am Dog.